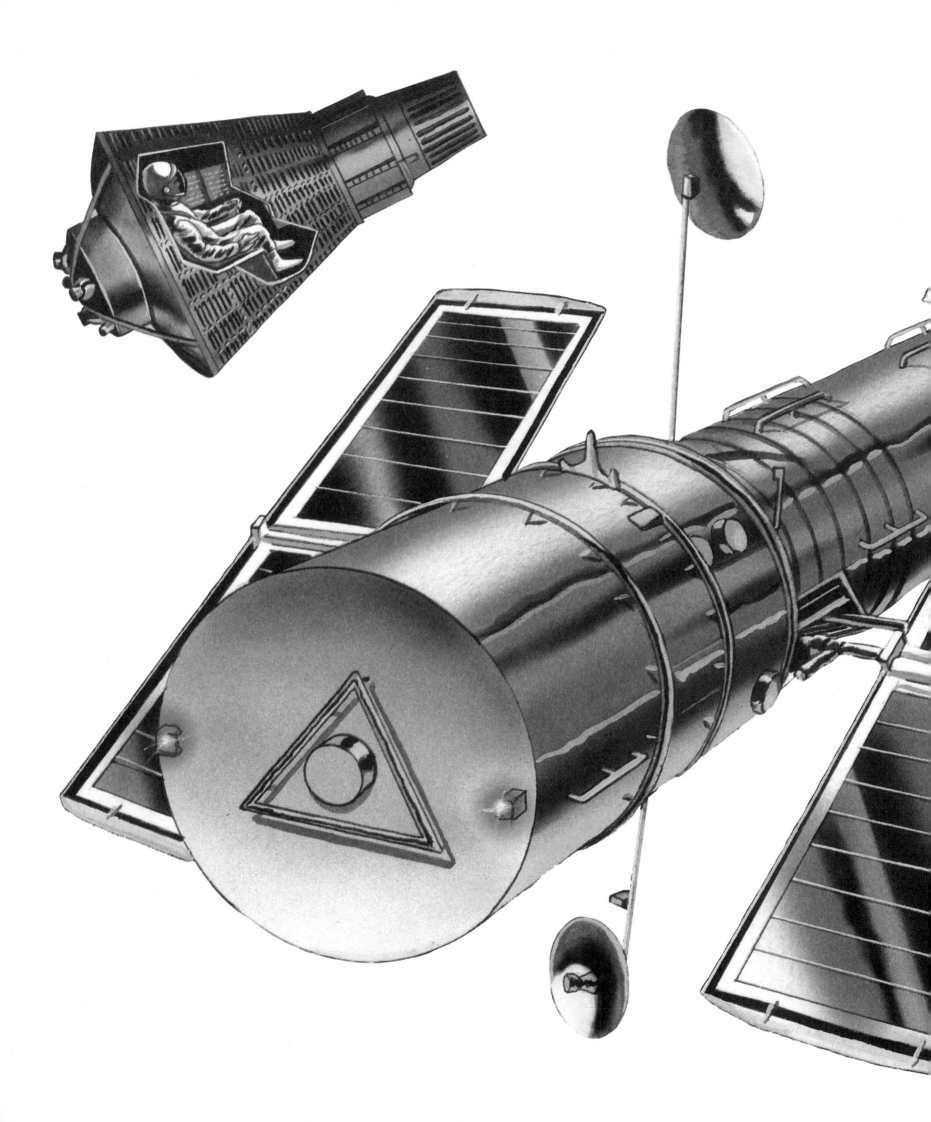

SPACE MACHINES

By Susan Abernathy • Illustrated by Tom LaPadula

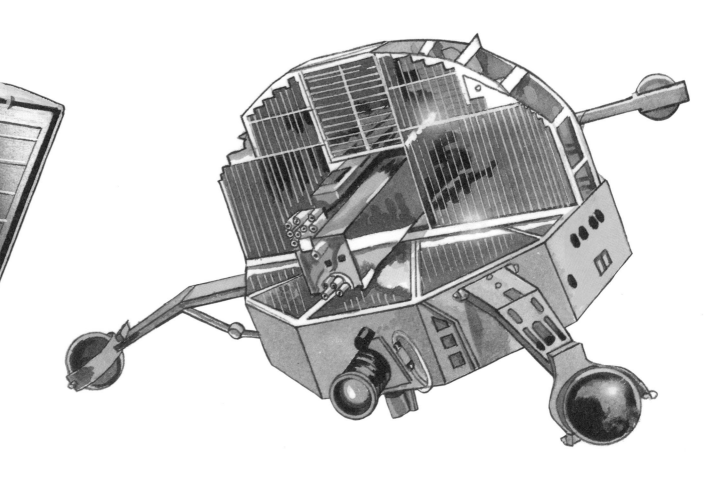

Editorial Adviser: Robert Haynes

Bibliography: A HISTORY OF SPACE FLIGHT by Eugene Emme, 1965, Holt, Rhinehart & Winston, Inc.; LIFT-OFF! by L. B. Taylor, Jr., 1968, E. P. Dutton, Inc.; EVENTS IN SPACE by Willy Ley, 1969, David McKay Company, Inc.; SATELLITES AND PROBES by Mitchell R. Sharpe, 1970, Doubleday & Company, Inc.; SPACE HISTORY by Tony Osman, 1983, St. Martin's Press; SPACEFARERS OF THE 80's & 90's: The Next Thousand People by Alcestis R. Oberg, 1985, Columbia University Press; INTRODUCTION TO SPACE: The Science of Spaceflight by Thomas Damon, 1989, Orbit Book Company.

A GOLDEN BOOK
Western Publishing Company, Inc., Racine, Wisconsin 53404

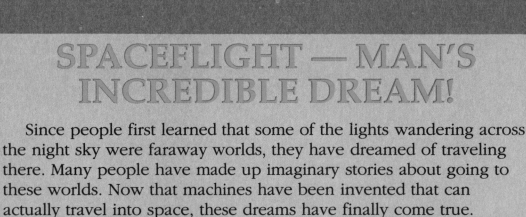

SPACEFLIGHT — MAN'S INCREDIBLE DREAM!

Since people first learned that some of the lights wandering across the night sky were faraway worlds, they have dreamed of traveling there. Many people have made up imaginary stories about going to these worlds. Now that machines have been invented that can actually travel into space, these dreams have finally come true.

Space machines have gone to all the planets in our solar system except Pluto. But before they could get into space, they had to escape Earth's **gravity**. Gravity is a powerful force throughout the universe. It is what holds things on the surface of our planet, and we can think of it is as a weight that keeps us on the Earth. Without gravity we would simply float into space.

To escape the Earth's gravity, space machines have to reach a very high speed. Think of a baseball. If you gently toss it up into the air, it quickly falls back down. But if you throw it very fast, it will stay in the air longer and go farther. Space machines need to go so fast, they will keep on flying until they reach space. There they can either keep on going to other worlds, or turn into an orbit around Earth.

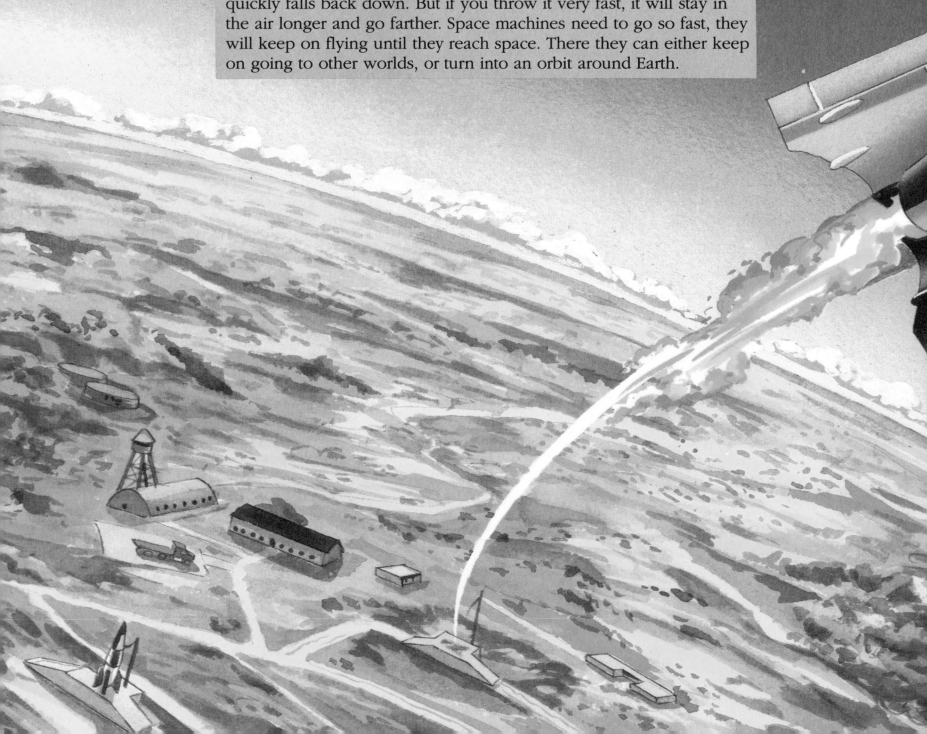

The *V-2* Rocket.
Both the United States and the Soviet Union based their military and civilian space rockets on the *V-2*. The first really successful American rocket was called *Redstone.* It was the one that literally got the space program off the ground.

ROCKETS

Rockets are the only machines fast and powerful enough to escape Earth's gravity. The basic idea behind rockets was first published in a magazine back in 1903. The author was a schoolteacher in Russia named Konstantin E. Tsiolkovsky (Con-STAN-teen Soil-COW-ski). He wrote about a machine that could blast off from Earth at a very high speed and could keep going as long as it had fuel to burn.

If you have ever blown up a balloon and let it go, you already know a little about rockets and their fuel. The air inside the balloon is actually fuel that sends the balloon flying around the room. When the air is used up, the balloon can no longer soar about.

Tsiolkovsky imagined rockets that had valves to control the flow of fuel. These rockets were able to speed up or slow down, and could even stop in mid-flight and start up again on their way to a space station or satellite.

Today rockets carry all sorts of things into space. Even the Space Shuttle uses a special kind of rocket power. In the early days of spaceflight one of the most popular rocket groups was called the Thor-based boosters. They launched many of the space machines you are going to read about in this book. Look for their names: *TIROS, OSO, Echo, Telstar,* and others.

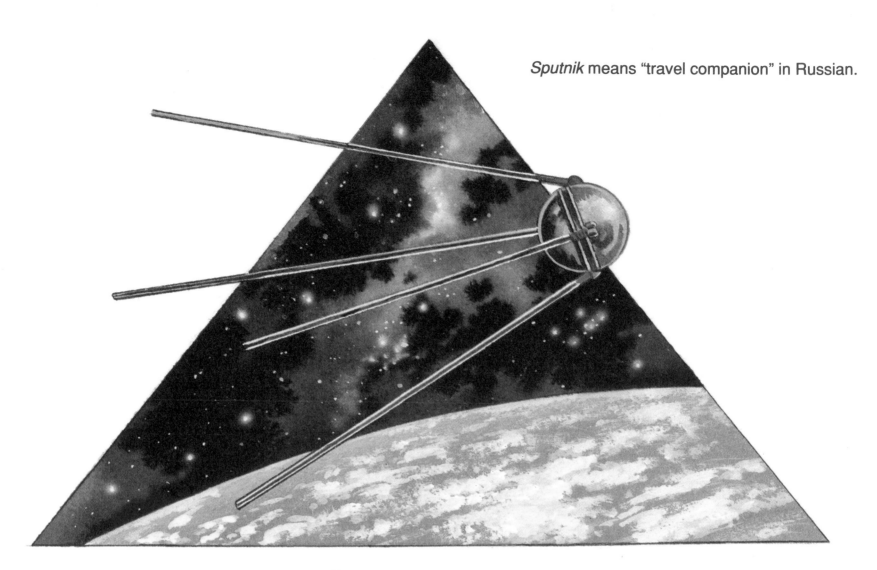

Sputnik means "travel companion" in Russian.

SATELLITES

Did you know Earth is a **satellite**? A satellite is any object in space that circles or revolves around a larger object. The Earth circles the sun, so it is a satellite. The moon is also a satellite because it circles the Earth. The path a satellite travels around an object is called the **orbit**.

There are two kinds of satellites: natural and artificial. The Earth and moon are **natural satellites**. Scientific, weather, communications, and navigational satellites are **artificial satellites** because they are man-made objects built specifically to orbit in space.

Sputnik (spoot-NIK) was the first artificial satellite. Launched by the Soviet Union on October 4, 1957, *Sputnik* was a 184-pound metal ball that orbited Earth every 96.2 minutes. It was carried into space atop a rocket. After the rocket put Sputnik in space, it fell back to Earth and burned up as it fell through the atmosphere. *Sputnik* remained in orbit for three months, sending its famous "bleep bleep" that was heard around the world. *Sputnik* finally fell back to Earth on January 4, 1958.

On November 3, 1957, the Soviets launched *Sputnik 2*, weighing 1,121 pounds and carrying Laika (LY-ka), a female dog whose name means "barker" in Russian. Laika lived in space for ten days. She died in orbit a week before the satellite fell back to Earth and burned up in the atmosphere. Her presence on *Sputnik 2* proved that an animal could live in space.

SPACE PROBES: TRAVELING MACHINES

When *Sputnik* was launched, humans had finally sent something into space! It started a space race, with both the Americans and the Soviets not only wanting to send machines into space, but also to go to the moon and other planets. To do so, both nations needed bigger and better space machines.

Neither the United States nor the Soviet Union knew what space would be like, so they both also needed **space probes**. These would be the machines they could send to objects in space and also use to gather information. For example, no one knew what was on the "dark side" of the moon. Because the moon turns around once each time it circles the Earth, it always keeps one side away from us. Space probes could be sent to look at what was there.

The first space probes were the *Luna* series, launched by the Soviets. *Luna 1* was launched on January 2, 1959, and it was intended to crash-land on the moon with its payload called *Mechta* (mitch-TAA), meaning "dream" in Russian. But *Luna 1* missed the moon and went into orbit around the sun. In all, the Soviets launched twenty-four *Luna* probes between 1959 and 1976. The *Luna* probes eventually hit the moon, sent back pictures of its dark side, and samples of moon soil. One probe even put a robot lunar rover, *Lunokhod* (loo-nac-HODE) on the moon.

The *Luna 3* space probe was the first artificial satellite to orbit around the moon.

9

WEATHER SATELLITES

Besides space probes that gather information about the sun and moon, we needed satellites to study the Earth. **Weather satellites** are artificial satellites whose major mission is to supply weather stations with pictures of clouds covering the Earth. These are the pictures you see every night on the evening weather report.

The first weather satellite was *TIROS 1*, launched by the United States on April 1, 1960. The letters in *TIROS* stand for **T**elevision **I**nfra**r**ed **O**bservational **S**atellite. Shaped like a hatbox, the *TIROS 1* satellite weighed 270 pounds, which is only an eighth of what today's weather satellites weigh. They have changed over the years into very complex machines.

Today we have two kinds of weather satellites. Polar orbiting satellites circle the world in a "sun-synchronous" orbit, meaning they pass over the same spot each day at the same time. The other kind of satellite is called a *GOES* satellite. *GOES* stands for **G**eostationary **O**perational **E**nvironmental **S**atellite. *GOES* have a "geosynchronous" orbit, which means they orbit so high above Earth that their orbit coincides with Earth's rotation. This gives them an appearance of continuously hovering over a single spot.

The next time you want to go to the beach, think o*f TIROS* and the other weather satellites that make it possible for us to tell a few days in advance if storms are coming.

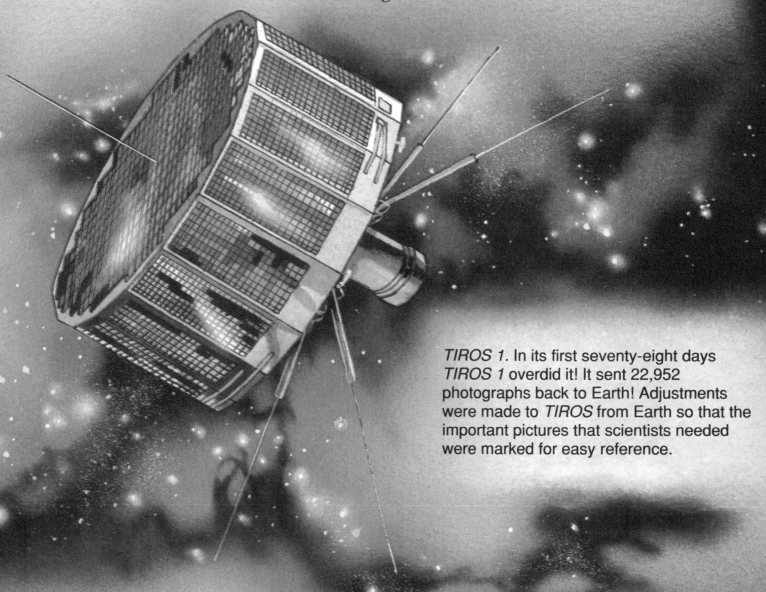

TIROS 1. In its first seventy-eight days *TIROS 1* overdid it! It sent 22,952 photographs back to Earth! Adjustments were made to *TIROS* from Earth so that the important pictures that scientists needed were marked for easy reference.

Navigational satellite. Early navigational satellites were in the Transit series. The Navy launched these satellites to help them track ships at sea.

NAVIGATIONAL SATELLITES

Satellites are also used to help boats and submarines find their way in bad weather. Ship captains normally follow maps that tell them the position of the sun and stars. This is how the captain tells where the ship is located on the vast ocean. In the past, ships often became lost at sea if there was heavy cloud cover or a storm.

Navigational satellites solve this problem. Like the *GOES,* these satellites stay high above the Earth in a geosynchronous orbit, keeping a fixed view on the surface below. They can send a radio signal to help guide ships at sea so captains don't have to worry if they can't see the sun or stars.

Before the Space Shuttle, navigational satellites helped find spacecraft and astronauts after splashdown. In those early days, when space missions were finished and the spacecraft returned to Earth, the capsules and astronauts landed in one of the Earth's oceans. The astronauts sent a signal from their module so a navigational satellite could track them and broadcast their location to a rescue ship in the area.

The *Orbiting Solar Observatory (OSO)* was sent up to study the sun. A satellite must travel at least 17,500 miles per hour to stay in orbit around Earth!

SCIENTIFIC SATELLITES

The job of **scientific satellites** is to study how the sun, the moon, and Earth and other planets of our solar system all work together. Sputnik was the first scientific satellite because its mission was to find out if signals could be sent through space to Earth.

In those beginning days of space exploration, scientific satellites were launched only by the Americans and the Soviets, and had names like Explorer, Vanguard, and Kosmos. But now countries all over the world launch scientific satellites with names like *Alouette* (Canada), *Ariel* (the United Kingdom), *San Marco* (Italy), and *Diademe* (France).

The first scientific satellite for the United States was *Explorer 1,* launched on January 31, 1958. *Explorer 1* weighed thirty pounds. On March 7, 1962, NASA (the **N**ational **A**eronautics and **S**pace **A**dministration) launched the first *Orbiting Solar Observatory,* or the *OSO-1.* The job of *OSO-1* was to study the sun, which it did very well. It worked for seventy-seven days and told us that the sun is 1 billion degrees Celsius at both poles and 30 million degrees Celsius in the solar flares.

Since these early satellites, the United States has launched other scientific satellites that have gone on to study the Earth's atmosphere, solar rays, and ultraviolet light. You'll read more about them in the following pages.

COMMUNICATIONS SATELLITES

Because of **communications satellites,** people all over the world can see or talk to one another in a matter of minutes. This was certainly not the case in 1815 when more than 2,000 British and American troops kept fighting a war that had been over for fifty-two days! That's how long it took the message of peace to reach them.

Earth's first communications satellite, however, is its natural satellite, the moon. In 1958, scientists sent voice transmissions from Holmdel, New Jersey, to the moon and then "reflected," or sent, the transmissions back to Goldstone, California.

But the first artificial communications satellite was *Echo 1*. It was launched by the United States on August 12, 1960. *Echo 1* was a balloon filled with gas and was 100 feet around. It was called Echo because that's exactly what it did, "echo" conversations back and forth. It orbited the Earth for eight years, until it finally gave in to gravity and burnt up in the Earth's atmosphere on May 24, 1968.

On July 10, 1962, the phone company sent its own communications satellite, *Telstar,* into space. It was designed and built by AT&T but launched by NASA. Unfortunately, *Telstar* disconnected itself because of a signal mixup and went dead. *Telstar 2* and *3* were launched soon afterward, and today there are communications satellites in space from countries all around the world.

Telstar 1.
To work properly, communications satellites must be in a geosynchronous orbit nearly 23,000 miles above the Earth. Today almost every major country has a communications satellite.

SPACE MACHINES FOR PEOPLE

Once artificial satellites went into space, people wanted to follow. But before humans could go, special space machines had to be built for them. These early spaceships were called **space capsules**. They were small, cramped, and cone-shaped, and rode on top of rockets that lifted them to space. These spaceships had to protect humans from space and keep them from burning up in the atmosphere when they returned to Earth.

Space is a rather unfriendly place. Down here on Earth we are used to having warmth from the sun, air to breathe, and water to drink. But space has none of these things. The Earth's **atmosphere** is what protects us from the harmful things in space.

Humans cannot live in space without an atmosphere to protect them. Both the United States and the Soviet Union designed programs to build machines and prepare people to go into space. Both countries named their space capsules after the names of their programs. In the United States the first space program and manned space capsules were called *Mercury*. In the Soviet Union the program and the machines were called *Vostok* (vos-TOCK). Americans who travel into space are called **astronauts**; Soviet space travelers are called **cosmonauts**.

14

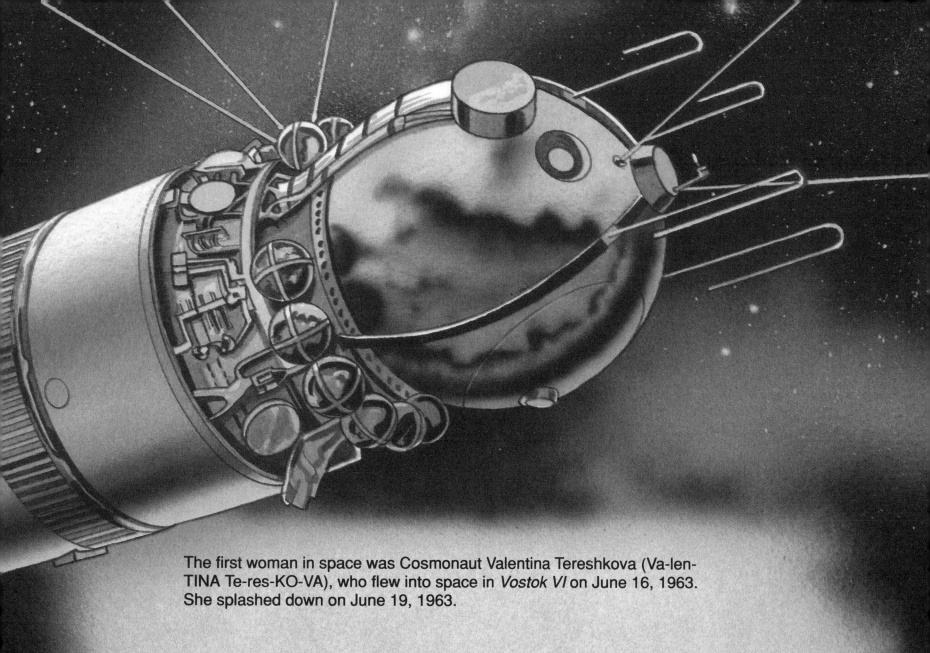

The first woman in space was Cosmonaut Valentina Tereshkova (Va-len-TINA Te-res-KO-VA), who flew into space in *Vostok VI* on June 16, 1963. She splashed down on June 19, 1963.

On April 12, 1961, Yuri Gagarin (You-RI Ga-GAR-in) was the first person to reach space. He was there for 108 minutes and made one complete orbit of the Earth in a space capsule called *Vostok 1*, which means "east" in Russian and was named after the first Soviet ship ever to sail around the globe (it sailed off in an easterly direction).

While in orbit, the cosmonaut drank and ate from small containers and practiced writing his observations down on a small tablet. He had to hold on to his writing table to keep it from floating away. Coming home, Yuri was ejected from the space capsule and landed separately with a big parachute. He landed in a field near a village, and the villagers rushed out to see him. The capsule landed nearby, charred and hot, but safe.

Soon afterward, the United States launched a man into space. On May 5, 1961, Lieutenant Commander Alan B. Shepard rode the *Mercury* space capsule, *Freedom 7,* to test the capsule and the Redstone booster rocket. He took off from Earth going 5,180 miles per hour and stayed in space for fifteen minutes, traveling 116 miles above the Earth. His capsule came down in the Atlantic Ocean, 302 miles from his starting point at Cape Canaveral, Florida. He recalled later that his flight was so hectic and short that he only had about thirty seconds to look out the window.

Mercury-Redstone 3
(*Mercury* space capsule and *Redstone* rocket) takes off from the launchpad at Cape Canaveral, Florida. This was the first manned spaceflight for the United States and sent Alan Shepard into space.

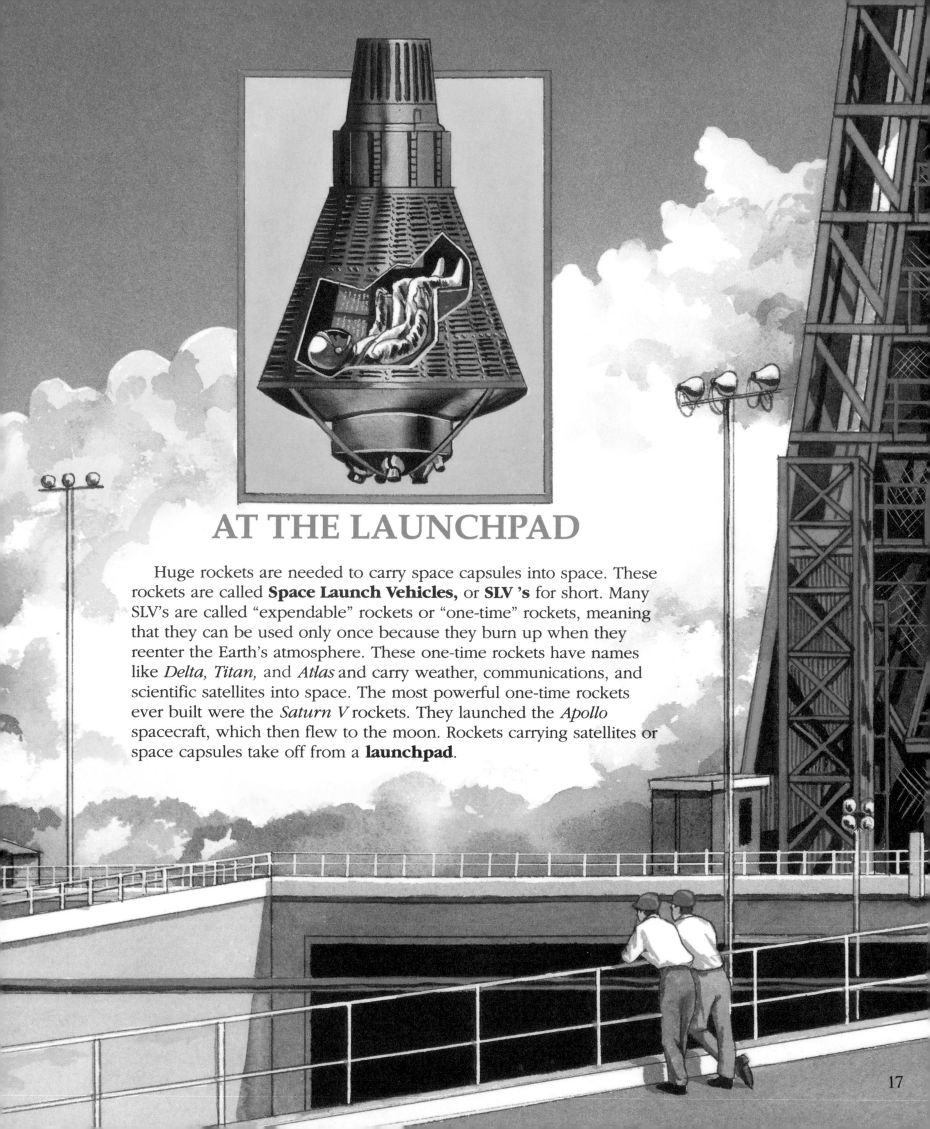

AT THE LAUNCHPAD

Huge rockets are needed to carry space capsules into space. These rockets are called **Space Launch Vehicles,** or **SLV's** for short. Many SLV's are called "expendable" rockets or "one-time" rockets, meaning that they can be used only once because they burn up when they reenter the Earth's atmosphere. These one-time rockets have names like *Delta, Titan,* and *Atlas* and carry weather, communications, and scientific satellites into space. The most powerful one-time rockets ever built were the *Saturn V* rockets. They launched the *Apollo* spacecraft, which then flew to the moon. Rockets carrying satellites or space capsules take off from a **launchpad**.

"3...2...1...LIFT-OFF!"

Not far from the launchpad is the **Launch Control Center.** This is where all the controls are located for monitoring the rocket and spacecraft before lift-off. The moment assigned for launch is called **"T" time** (**"T"** for **takeoff**). Time is counted backward to this moment. So if a spaceflight is scheduled eight hours away, it is referred to as "T-minus eight hours and counting." This is known as the **countdown**.

The time from when a rocket takes off until it reaches its orbit is known as **lift-off**. Lift-off can be a dangerous time. If the rocket does not get enough power to overcome gravity, it can fall back to Earth.

The time from a successful lift-off until the machines enter space is the **orbiting period**. This is the time when the rocket pushes the spacecraft into the right path to orbit the Earth or to continue its journey to another planet.

The Launch Control Center at Cape Canaveral, Florida, during the launch of *Mercury, Atlas 6*. This was John Glenn's historic orbital flight on board the *Friendship 7 Mercury* capsule.

The *Mercury* capsule *Friendship 7* during its fiery reentry.

RETURNING FROM SPACE

Another dangerous stage of manned spaceflight is **reentry**. This stage happens when a spacecraft of any kind passes back through the Earth's atmosphere after flying in space. Reentry is dangerous because, as a space capsule leaves its orbit in space to return to Earth, gases and other particles in the atmosphere cause the surface of the space capsule to become extremely hot. The early space capsules had extra-thick walls to shield them from the heat. During reentry the outside of the capsules could burst into flames, but the crew and the inside of the capsule would be protected.

Although scientists studied the information from instruments inside the flown capsules, the capsules could not be sent into space again. In the 1970's the Space Shuttle was developed to solve this problem. It was the first spaceship for humans that could be used over and over. Special tiles were made that could stand the heat of reentry and protect the astronauts.

LANDING IN THE OCEAN

Early in the space program, the final stages of a spaceflight were called **splashdown** and **recovery**. Long before a rocket and space capsule went into space, the landing place for the capsule was picked. This was because ships, airplanes, helicopters, and even satellites had to know where to go to find the space capsule and the astronauts.

After passing through much of the atmosphere, the space capsule opened a big parachute to slow it down before hitting the ocean. This moment was called splashdown. Special signals were relayed from the space capsule to a navigational satellite high above the Earth. The satellite sent another signal to a naval ship waiting nearby to pick up the astronauts. After the astronauts were safely on the naval ship, the capsule was picked up by a military helicopter and carried back to the space center. When a capsule had been safely picked up by the helicopter, the moment was called recovery.

Marine Corps Sikorsky *UH-34* recovery helicopter retrieving the *Friendship 7* space capsule from the ocean.

The first space walk was by cosmonaut Aleksei Leonov
(A-LEK-say Lee-o-NOV) from the *Voskhod 2* (vosc-HODE)
space capsule on March 18,1965. He spent twenty minutes in
space. The first U.S. space walk was by astronaut Edward White
on June 3, 1965, and lasted twenty-two minutes. At NASA, a space
walk is called **EVA**, which stands for **e**xtra**v**ehicular **a**ctivity.

A WALK IN SPACE

Beyond Earth's atmosphere, or protective layer, is space. It is very
cold in shadows and very hot in direct sunlight, and it has no air
pressure. When astronauts leave their capsule to go for a space walk,
they must wear a **space suit**. Space suits are just another kind of
space machine. They work in much the same way as space capsules.
They are designed to give an astronaut some of the air pressure a
person would feel on Earth. Space suits also supply warmth and
oxygen for astronauts to breathe and constantly check on their heart
rate and blood pressure. If there is a problem, a tone is signaled to
the astronaut through headphones and the astronaut adjusts the space
suit.

Today's space suits have a backpack that contains two oxygen
tanks, a fan to keep air circulating inside the suit, an air filter to clean
up any toxic gases that can form inside the suit, and a battery pack
that can last up to seven hours.

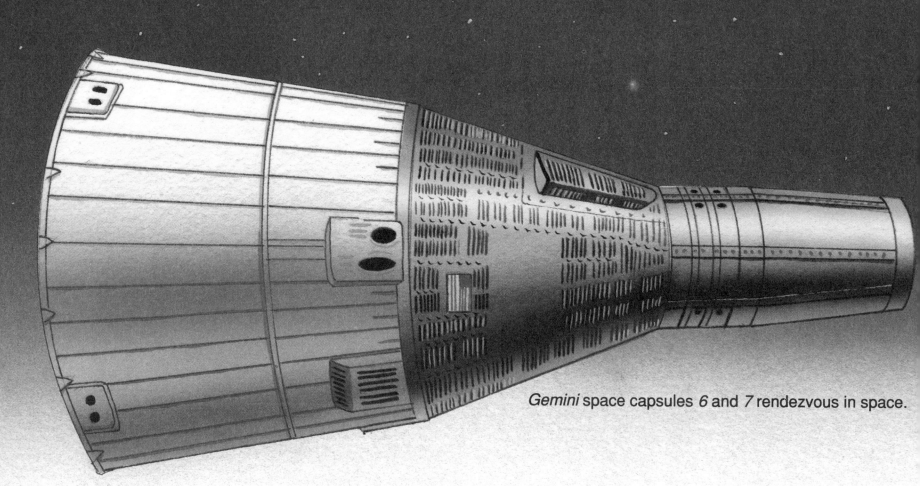

Gemini space capsules *6* and *7* rendezvous in space.

MEETING IN SPACE

Sometimes spacecraft need to meet other spacecraft in space, or to land on another planet. The two maneuvers spacecraft use to do this are called **rendezvous** and **docking**.

When two moving objects meet in space, it is called a rendezvous. In a rendezvous, the two objects don't touch, they just come very close. When two objects do touch, it is called **docking**.

The first rendezvous was by the U.S. *Gemini* space capsules 6 and 7 in 1965. The two space capsules met 188 miles above Earth. It was done by computers and control panels, inside the spacecraft, that were automatically set before launching.

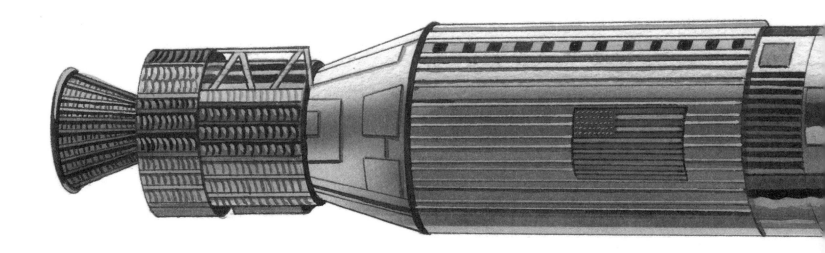

It is not easy to rendezvous, but it is even harder to dock. The two objects must be lined up perfectly and must come together very gently to avoid a crash. Unlike a rendezvous, which is done automatically by the space capsule's computer, docking is done manually by the crew. Once two ships have rendezvoused, the astronauts take over and ease the ships into locking position to dock. In 1975, the first docking in space was done by Americans and Soviets in the *Apollo-Soyuz* Test Project.

The *Gemini 8* space capsule docking with an *Agena* rocket in orbit high above Earth.

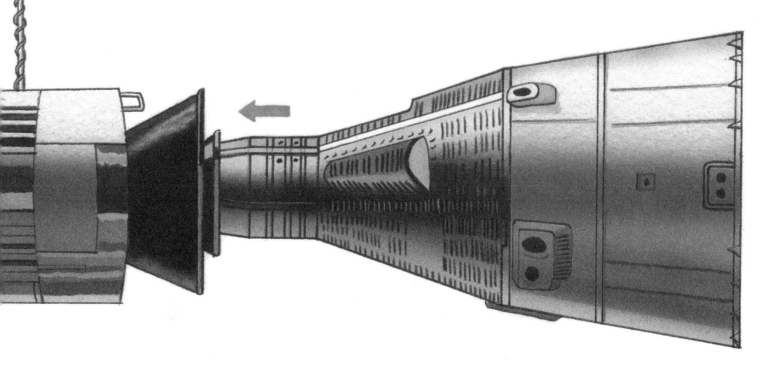

The **Lunar Excursion Module** (LEM) descends from *Apollo 11*'s Command Module in orbit around the moon.

MAN ON THE MOON

In 1961, President John F. Kennedy challenged NASA. By the end of the decade, he wanted NASA to land a man on the moon and bring him back safely. When NASA started the moon-landing program, it was called Project Apollo. All the space capsules involved in getting men to the moon were called *Apollo*. Some missions in the Apollo program didn't go anywhere near the moon but practiced important space maneuvers like rendezvous and docking. From 1968 to 1972, three manned flights orbited around the moon (*Apollo 8, 10,* and *13*) and six landed (*Apollo 11, 12, 14, 15, 16,* and *17*).

The *Apollo* space capsule was made up of five different units: the **Command Module, Service Module, Lunar Excursion Module** (or **LEM**), the **Lunar Module Adapter,** and the **Launch Escape System.** Each *Apollo* spacecraft stood about 83 feet high, and was always launched atop *Saturn V* rockets. Together, the spacecraft and the *Saturn V* rocket stood nearly 400 feet tall on the launchpad!

The Command Module was the only unit of the spacecraft that returned to Earth. It housed the crew's living quarters and was where the crew stayed during reentry into the Earth's atmosphere. The Command Module was shaped like a cone. The bottom was 13.8 feet across, and the inside measured only 11 feet 5 inches high, coming to a point at the top. The small space inside was meant to hold three astronauts. Pure oxygen was sent through the life-support system, and the capsule was kept at a temperature of 75°F.

The Service Module housed all the electrical controls for the space capsule. The Lunar Module Adapter connected the space capsule to the *Saturn V* rocket and was 28 feet tall and 12.8 feet around.

The **L**unar **E**xcursion **M**odule (LEM) of the *Apollo 11* spacecraft landed on the moon at 4:18 p.m., Eastern Daylight Time, July 20, 1969. Almost seven hours later, at 10:56 p.m., Astronaut Neil A. Armstrong set foot on the moon and spoke these famous words: "That's one small step for [a] man; one giant leap for mankind."

27

EXPLORING THE MOON'S SURFACE

The Lunar Excursion Module had a very special job. It had to land gently on the surface of the moon, take off again, and return its passengers safely to the *Apollo* Command Module orbiting above. The LEM was the unit that actually landed on the moon's surface. It had two windows for the astronauts to see out of and a tube for them to enter and leave the module. It had four legs for support.

Another space machine made just for exploring the moon's surface was the Lunar Roving Vehicle or the LRV. The LRV was a battery-powered car that allowed the astronauts to travel away from the landing place to pick up samples of moon rocks. The LRV was carried into space on three separate *Apollo* flights and was put together on the moon's surface.

The *Apollo 11* mission, which landed the first men on the moon, lasted 195 hours, 18 minutes, and 35 seconds, or just a little more than eight days from lift-off to splashdown.

On the *Apollo 11* moon flight, the Command Module was named the *Columbia,* and the Lunar Excursion Module was named the *Eagle.* The *Eagle* could not lift off from the moon until the *Columbia* was almost directly overhead. Then the *Eagle* could use its fuel to lift off, rendezvous, and dock with *Columbia.*

After a successful reentry, the *Columbia* and its crew splashed down in the Pacific Ocean at 12:51 p.m., EDT, just thirteen nautical miles from the recovery ship, the U.S.S. *Hornet.*

The Apollo program ended in 1975 with history's first international spaceflight when an *Apollo* capsule docked with a Russian two-man spacecraft, the *Soyuz* (Soy-UTS). There were many technical problems to solve before this could be done, and after much discussion, it was decided that the *Apollo* space capsule would have a special adapter that could connect to the *Soyuz.* For nearly two days the astronauts and cosmonauts moved back and forth between the two spaceships and did experiments together.

SPACE PROBES: PLANET DETECTIVES

After astronauts successfully landed on the moon, scientists became even more curious about the other planets in our solar system. During the late 1970's and early 1980's better satellites and space probes were built.

New space probes could travel the incredible distances to other planets. They could land on planets by using rendezvous and docking techniques, fly through the solar system, take pictures of the planets' surfaces, and gather important information.

One probe, *Pioneer 10*, has even left the solar system and is now gathering information on the universe beyond. *Pioneer 10* was launched in 1972 and was the first probe to fly past Jupiter. *Pioneer* was only supposed to last a little over a year and a half, but it just kept on going. Some writers have even nicknamed it "the little spacecraft that could." It was still going strong eleven years later, on June 13, 1983, when it sent back information that it had left the solar system. To this day it is still sending signals.

The *Pioneer 10* space probe takes pictures of the planet Jupiter. Following this encounter, *Pioneer* would fly on to cross the orbit of the most distant planet, which, on July 13, 1983, was Neptune. This made *Pioneer 10* the first spacecraft ever to leave the solar system.

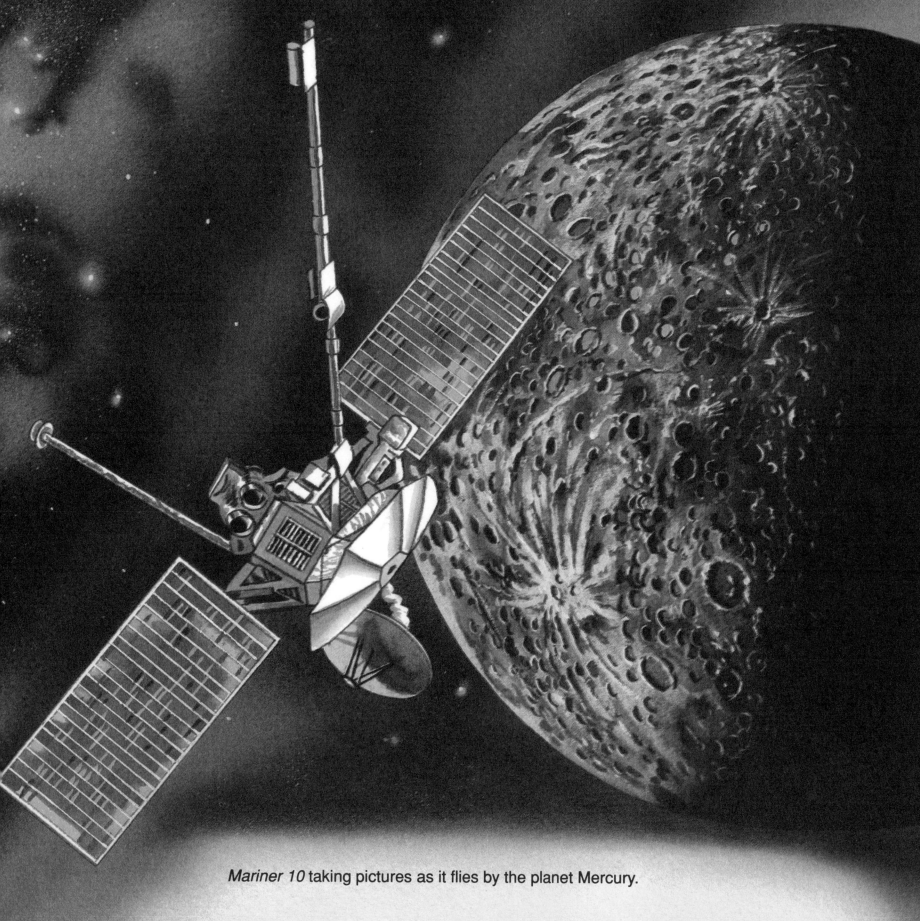

Mariner 10 taking pictures as it flies by the planet Mercury.

Another famous space probe was *Mariner 10*. It was launched on November 1, 1973, and it flew by Venus in January 1974. Three weeks after it flew by Venus, *Mariner 10* flew by the planet Mercury.

    Mariner 10 was the first space probe to reach Mercury, the planet closest to the sun. It took close-up photographs of Mercury's surface and instantly sent them back to Earth. It stopped transmitting on March 16, 1975.

31

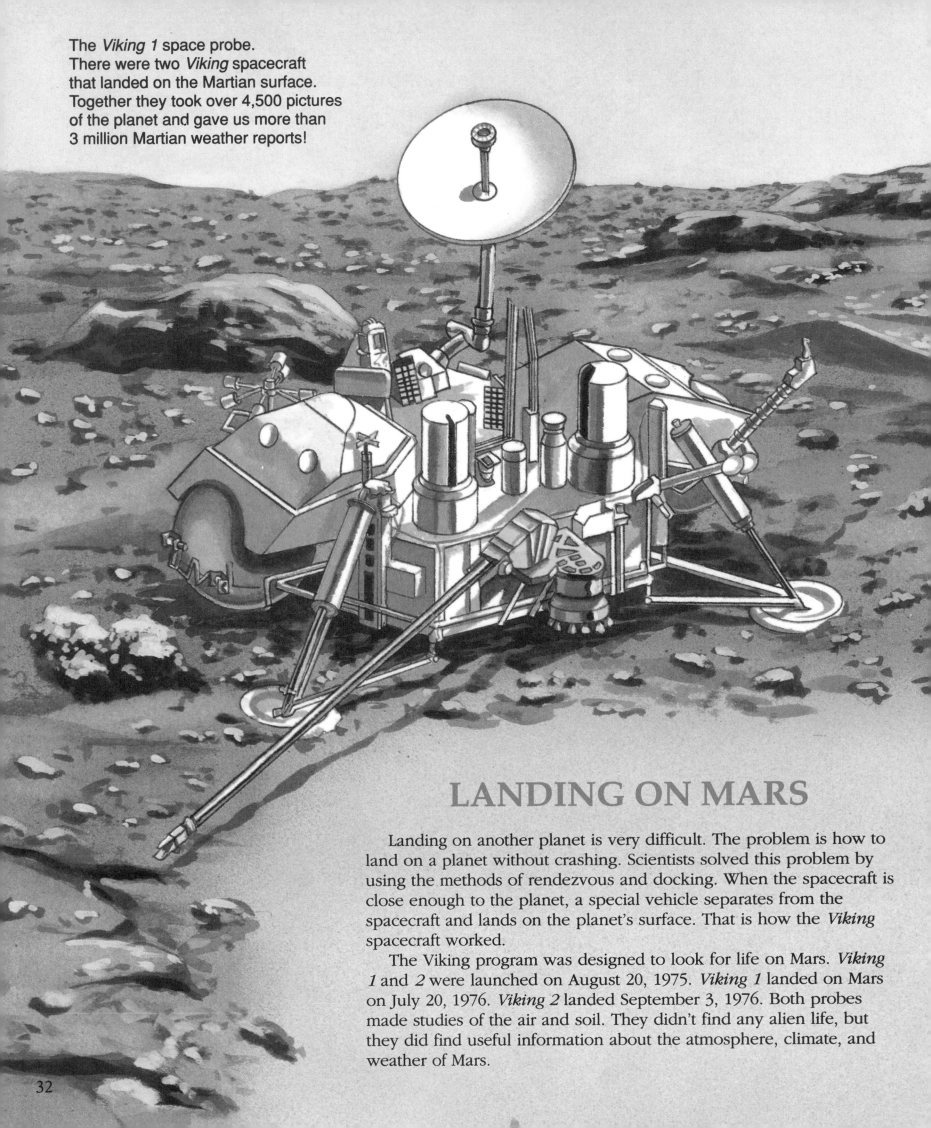

The *Viking 1* space probe. There were two *Viking* spacecraft that landed on the Martian surface. Together they took over 4,500 pictures of the planet and gave us more than 3 million Martian weather reports!

LANDING ON MARS

Landing on another planet is very difficult. The problem is how to land on a planet without crashing. Scientists solved this problem by using the methods of rendezvous and docking. When the spacecraft is close enough to the planet, a special vehicle separates from the spacecraft and lands on the planet's surface. That is how the *Viking* spacecraft worked.

The Viking program was designed to look for life on Mars. *Viking 1* and *2* were launched on August 20, 1975. *Viking 1* landed on Mars on July 20, 1976. *Viking 2* landed September 3, 1976. Both probes made studies of the air and soil. They didn't find any alien life, but they did find useful information about the atmosphere, climate, and weather of Mars.

GIOTTO: INSIDE HALLEY'S COMET

In the summer of 1985, the European Space Agency's spacecraft *Giotto* was launched to look at Halley's Comet. It met up with the comet on March 14, 1986, and flew closer to the comet's center than any other spacecraft. Its mission was very hard. Even though *Giotto* survived its encounter, it was knocked out by comet dust for almost a half hour. All but two of its instruments were hit. Even so, *Giotto* did well. It saw that the very solid middle part of the comet was shaped like a peanut and that its surface was very dark in color.

Other probes were also sent to look at Halley's Comet. The Soviet Union sent *Vega 1* and 2. Their cameras were able to take very clear pictures of details on the comet's surface. Japan also sent two probes, the *Suisei* (Sue-say), which means "comet," and the *Sakigaki* (SA-ku-GA-ki), which means "pioneer." These probes took pictures of the bright, gaseous lights that surround Halley's solid middle.

All these spacecraft sent back so much information about Halley's Comet that scientists all around the world are still finding out new things about it and other comets.

The *Giotto* probe. Even though *Giotto* was hit by a lot of comet dust and solar wind, it was able to look at the very solid middle of Halley's Comet and find out its shape and color.

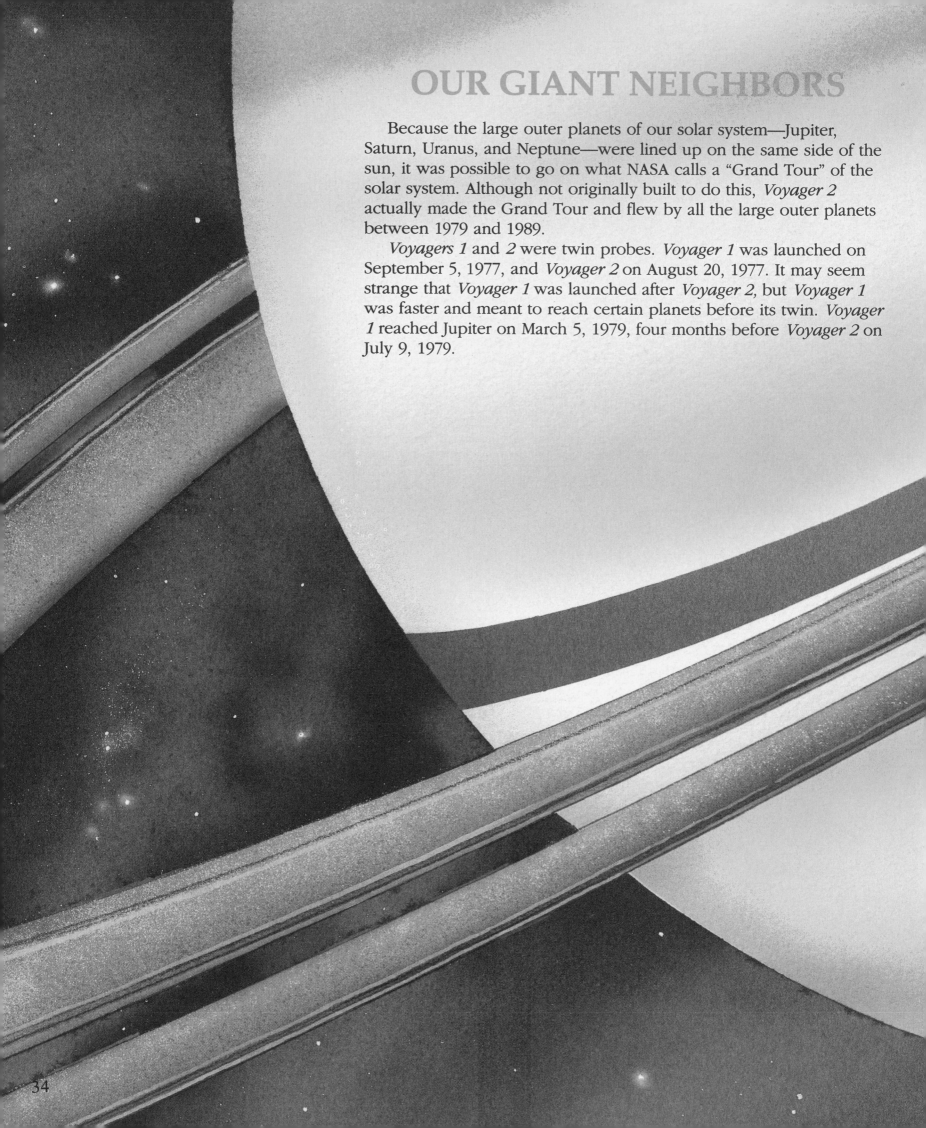

OUR GIANT NEIGHBORS

Because the large outer planets of our solar system—Jupiter, Saturn, Uranus, and Neptune—were lined up on the same side of the sun, it was possible to go on what NASA calls a "Grand Tour" of the solar system. Although not originally built to do this, *Voyager 2* actually made the Grand Tour and flew by all the large outer planets between 1979 and 1989.

Voyagers 1 and *2* were twin probes. *Voyager 1* was launched on September 5, 1977, and *Voyager 2* on August 20, 1977. It may seem strange that *Voyager 1* was launched after *Voyager 2*, but *Voyager 1* was faster and meant to reach certain planets before its twin. *Voyager 1* reached Jupiter on March 5, 1979, four months before *Voyager 2* on July 9, 1979.

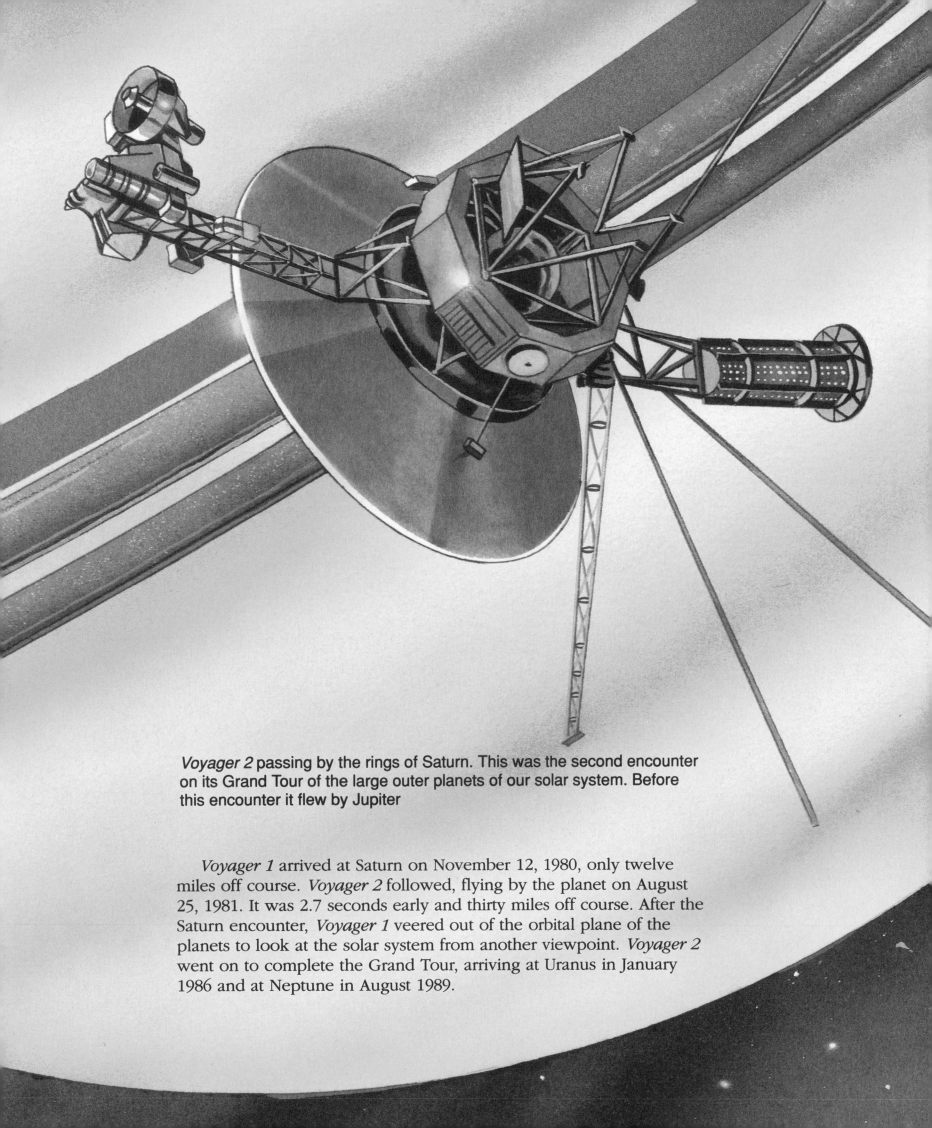

Voyager 2 passing by the rings of Saturn. This was the second encounter on its Grand Tour of the large outer planets of our solar system. Before this encounter it flew by Jupiter

Voyager 1 arrived at Saturn on November 12, 1980, only twelve miles off course. *Voyager 2* followed, flying by the planet on August 25, 1981. It was 2.7 seconds early and thirty miles off course. After the Saturn encounter, *Voyager 1* veered out of the orbital plane of the planets to look at the solar system from another viewpoint. *Voyager 2* went on to complete the Grand Tour, arriving at Uranus in January 1986 and at Neptune in August 1989.

COMMUNICATIONS SATELLITES TODAY: A SMALLER WORLD

In 1965, a group of countries formed an organization called Intelsat that launched a new communications satellite, the *Early Bird*. Intelsat stands for **In**ternational **Tel**ecommunications **Sat**ellites and was created to provide satellite communications to all the nations of the world. The *Early Bird* is known technically as *Intelsat 1*. By 1985, some 170 countries belonged to Intelsat.

Early Bird was important because it was the first communications satellite to provide services to citizens and not just government agencies and the military. The *Early Bird* could either send phone calls or TV pictures, but not both at the same time. Since then, the Intelsat network has launched more than fifteen satellites into space. These are more advanced and can supply both phone and television services to many countries.

When the next Olympic games are on TV, think of the *Intelsat* satellites sending the pictures almost instantly!

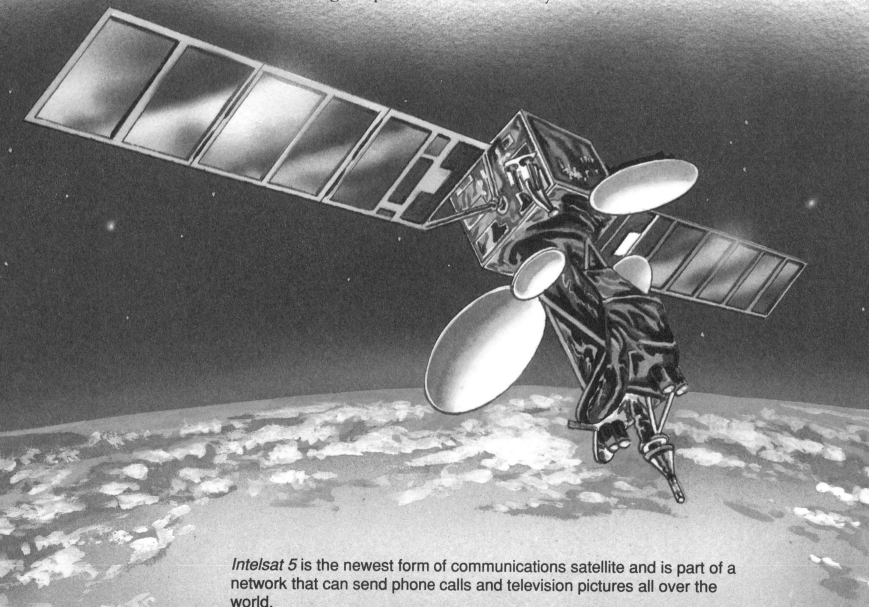

Intelsat 5 is the newest form of communications satellite and is part of a network that can send phone calls and television pictures all over the world.

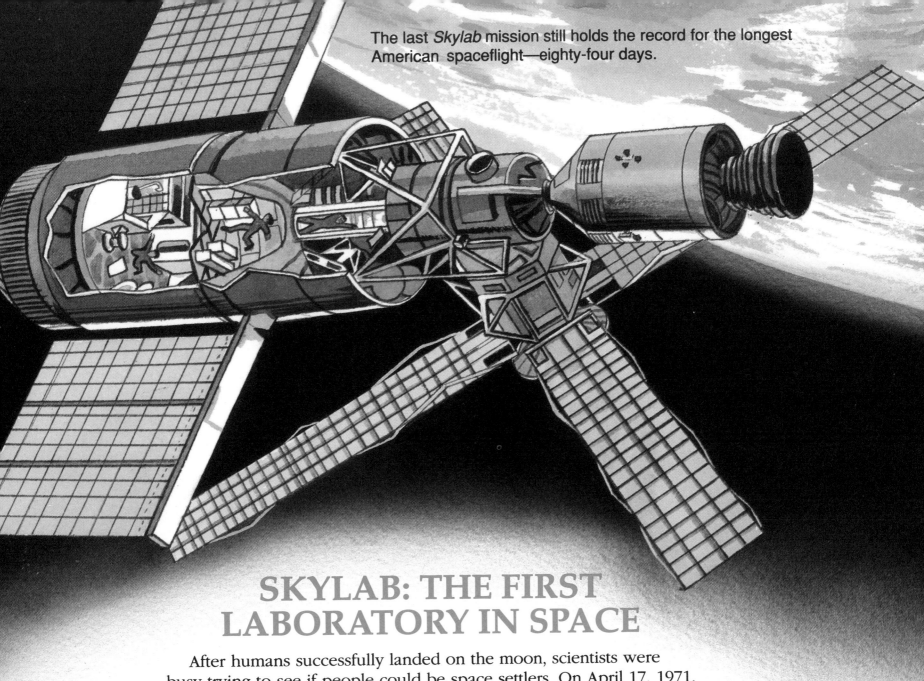

The last *Skylab* mission still holds the record for the longest American spaceflight—eighty-four days.

SKYLAB: THE FIRST LABORATORY IN SPACE

After humans successfully landed on the moon, scientists were busy trying to see if people could be space settlers. On April 17, 1971, the Soviet Union launched the very first **space station** and called it *Salyut* (SAL-UTS).

On May 14, 1973, NASA launched the first U.S. space station, *Skylab,* into an orbit 275 miles above the Earth. It held three astronauts. The idea behind *Skylab* was to have astronauts live on a spaceship and eat, sleep, listen to music, and play games. It may sound like a vacation, but the astronauts had to work, too, doing scientific experiments.

Most of the astronauts only stayed on the spaceship for a brief time, maybe two or three weeks. Then they came back to Earth. Since this was before the Space Shuttle, crews and supplies were taken to *Skylab* by *Apollo* spacecraft. The Command Module would rendezvous and dock with *Skylab*.

Skylab was not meant to be a permanent space station. It was supposed to only last nine years, but soon NASA discovered that *Skylab's* orbit was too low. It was constantly being slowed down by very thin traces of atmosphere. Finally, in the summer of 1979, six years after its launching, *Skylab* crashed to Earth. As it fell it broke into pieces. A seventeen-year-old Australian boy claimed a $10,000 prize for finding the first "official" piece of *Skylab*.

37

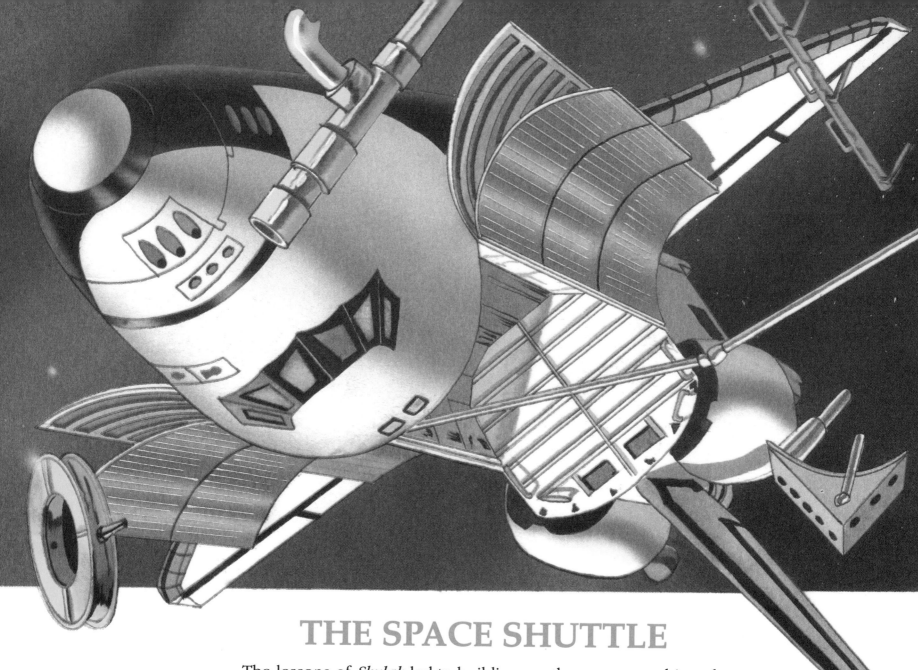

THE SPACE SHUTTLE

The lessons of *Skylab* led to building another space machine, the **Space Shuttle**. It was the first spaceship designed to orbit the Earth, come back, and be reused. What we sometimes think of as the Space Shuttle is really only a part of it called the **orbiter**. This is the part that looks like an airplane; it has wings and can glide through the air. But the orbiter is only part of an entire **Space Transportation System,** or **STS**. The rest of the STS is made up of the large fuel tank, the main engines on the tail of the orbiter, and the two solid-fuel rocket boosters, placed on each side of the fuel tank.

The first STS was launched on April 12, 1981. Four Space Shuttles operated between 1981 and 1986—*Columbia, Challenger, Discovery,* and *Atlantis*. On January 26, 1986, an explosion occurred on the Space Shuttle *Challenger,* seventy-four seconds after lift-off. The explosion killed all seven crew members, including the first schoolteacher in space, Christa McAuliffe. After this tragedy, shuttle flights were postponed until September 1988, when *Discovery* was launched on a successful five-day mission.

The Soviet Union has also developed a space shuttle similar to the American model. It made its first unmanned test flight in November 1988.

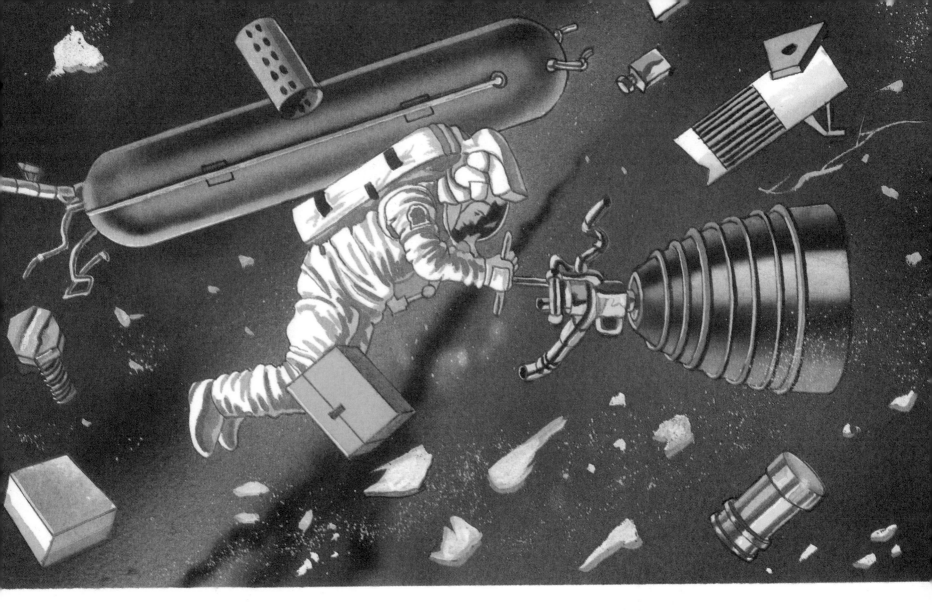

Imagine what it would look like if the Space Shuttle astronauts tried to clean up all the junk in space!

JUNK IN SPACE

Space pollution or **space junk** is becoming a very serious problem. Once an object reaches its orbit, it stays there unless something forces it back to Earth. Some satellites and pieces of rockets have been in space for thirty years. During the first ten years after the launch of *Sputnik,* 136 spacecraft never obtained their orbit and are still floating in space! Over 2,940 known items are still floating in space.

In 1988 NASA listed over 4 million pounds of material orbiting the Earth and two million of it was space junk! NASA listed the material as follows: 2,000 spacecraft; 5,000 large objects that have broken off from various spacecraft; 30,000 baseball-and marble-sized objects; and over 100,000 objects that are the size of paint chips or smaller.

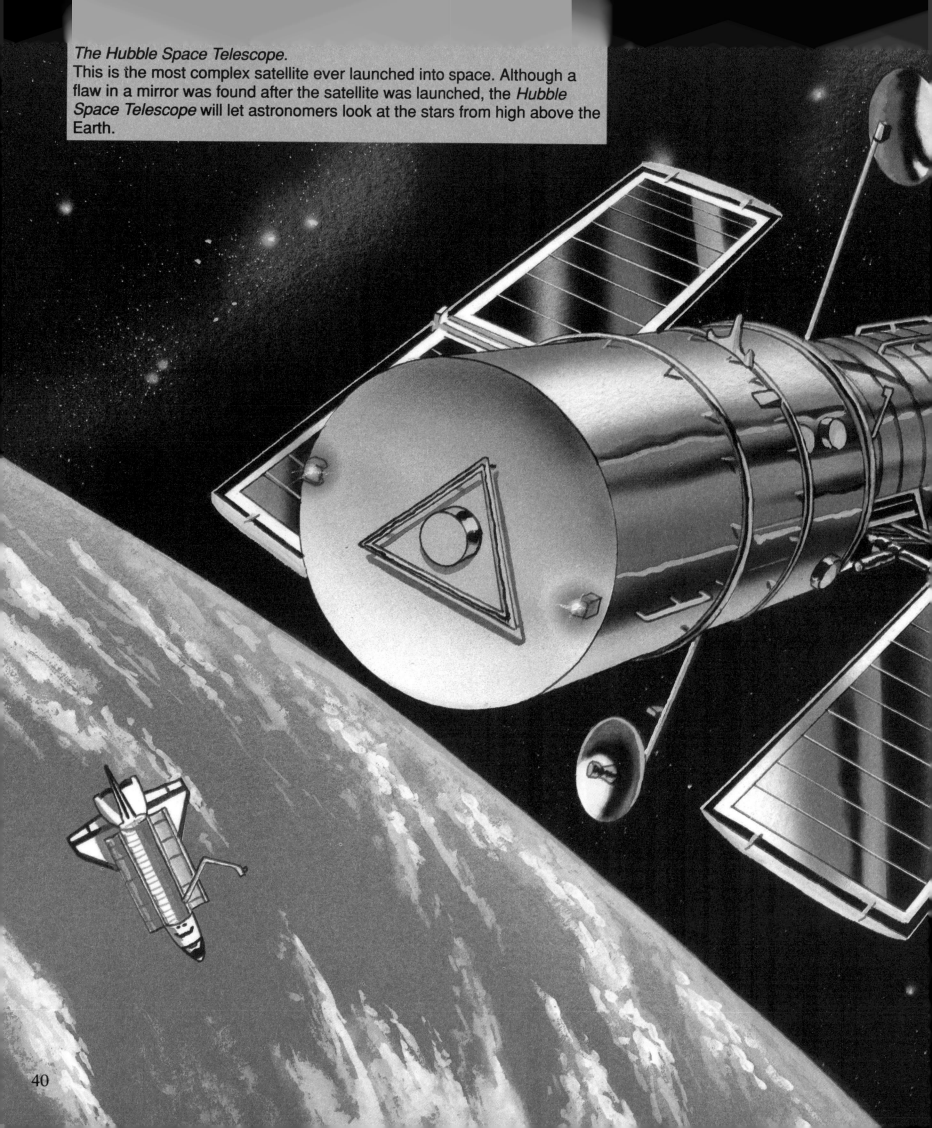

The Hubble Space Telescope.
This is the most complex satellite ever launched into space. Although a flaw in a mirror was found after the satellite was launched, the *Hubble Space Telescope* will let astronomers look at the stars from high above the Earth.

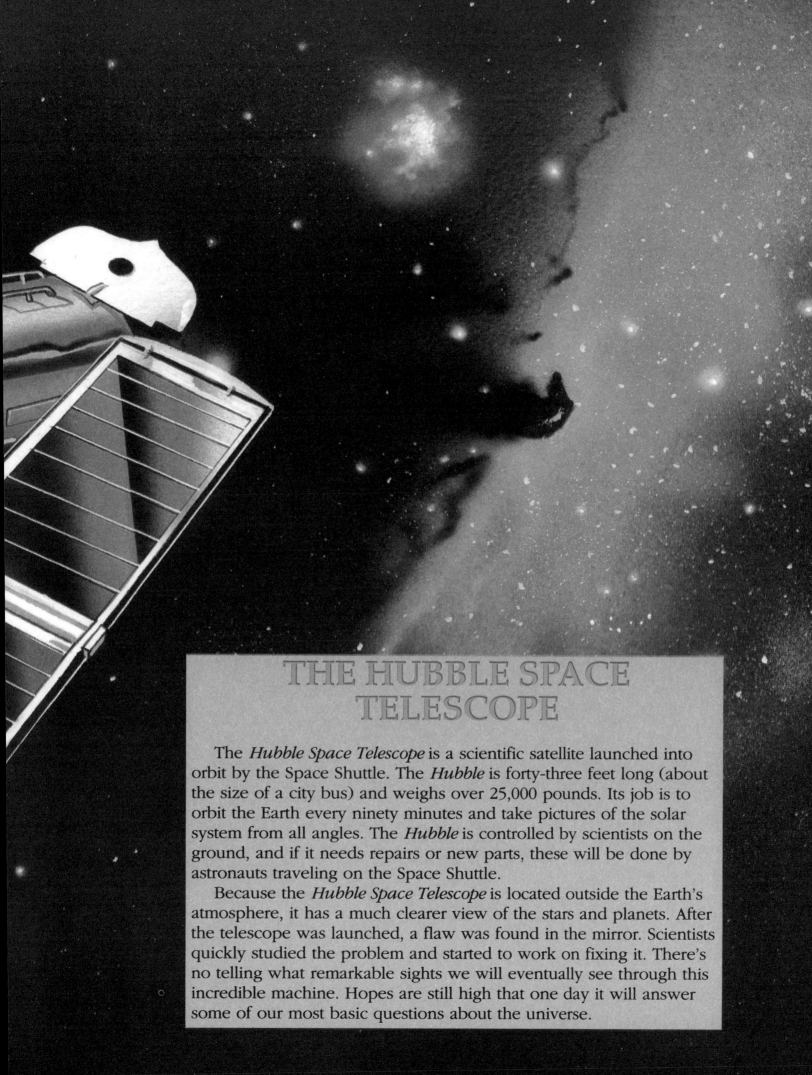

THE HUBBLE SPACE TELESCOPE

The *Hubble Space Telescope* is a scientific satellite launched into orbit by the Space Shuttle. The *Hubble* is forty-three feet long (about the size of a city bus) and weighs over 25,000 pounds. Its job is to orbit the Earth every ninety minutes and take pictures of the solar system from all angles. The *Hubble* is controlled by scientists on the ground, and if it needs repairs or new parts, these will be done by astronauts traveling on the Space Shuttle.

Because the *Hubble Space Telescope* is located outside the Earth's atmosphere, it has a much clearer view of the stars and planets. After the telescope was launched, a flaw was found in the mirror. Scientists quickly studied the problem and started to work on fixing it. There's no telling what remarkable sights we will eventually see through this incredible machine. Hopes are still high that one day it will answer some of our most basic questions about the universe.

The *Mir* Space Station.
NASA also has plans for a permanent space station called *Freedom*,
and it will be in space by the late 1990's.

SPACE STATIONS

The space station of the 90's will provide a permanent scientific community in space. The U.S. Space Station *Freedom* will be like a small laboratory orbiting the Earth, and scientists will be busy at work discovering new ways to make our life on Earth even more enjoyable. *Freedom* will also provide platforms where Space Shuttles and satellites can dock. There will be special rooms called observatories where the Earth below and the universe beyond can be viewed.

The first permanent space station is already in orbit. It is called *Mir* (MEER) and was launched by the Soviet Union on February 19, 1986. Space stations like *Mir* and the United States's *Freedom* might be the first stop on a trip to the moon, Mars, or beyond!

SPACE COLONIES: SPACE MACHINES OF THE FUTURE

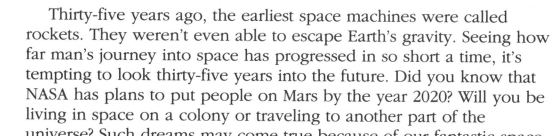

Thirty-five years ago, the earliest space machines were called rockets. They weren't even able to escape Earth's gravity. Seeing how far man's journey into space has progressed in so short a time, it's tempting to look thirty-five years into the future. Did you know that NASA has plans to put people on Mars by the year 2020? Will you be living in space on a colony or traveling to another part of the universe? Such dreams may come true because of our fantastic space machines!

43

Glossary of Space Terms

Astronaut — American term for persons who travel in space.

Atmosphere — The air around the Earth. It is also the gases and particles that surround or make up other planets.

Brain — The control system of any spacecraft.

Chicken switch — The emergency escape lever located near an astronaut's left knee.

Cosmonaut: — Soviet term for persons who travels in space.

Doghouse — Small compartments on the outside of rockets that house machinery or instruments.

EVA — Stands for Extravehicular Activity. Any movement outside a spacecraft, like a space walk.

Gravity — A force that exerts a pull on all objects on Earth.

Launchpad — A place where rockets and spacecraft take off.

LRV — Lunar Roving Vehicle. A jeep-like machine for driving on the moon's surface.

Recovery — When a spacecraft is retrieved and returned to the space center after a flight in space.

Reentry — When a spacecraft passes back through the atmosphere to return to Earth after a spaceflight.

Rocket — A space machine that travels fast enough to break through Earth's gravity.

Satellite: — Any object, natural or man-made, that circles around another larger object in space.

SLV — Space Launch Vehicles. Powerful rockets that launch satellites and capsules into space.

Splashdown — When a space capsule falls into the ocean after reentry from a space mission.

Space capsule — Space machines that carry people into space.

Space probe — A form of artificial, scientific satellite meant for travel in our solar system and beyond.

Space Shuttle — A reusable spacecraft that is sent into space on rockets and returns to Earth like an airplane.

STS — Space Transportation System. The full name of the Space Shuttle.

"T" time — The launch time for a rocket or spacecraft.

Zip fuel — High-energy, jet-engine fuel.

Index